FORBIDDEN STORIES OF AN IMMIGRANT

To a very well known friend for years. Enjoy and you won't need comments. gladiusbooks@gmail.com

FORBIDDEN STORIES OF AN IMMIGRANT

Phern H.

Translated by: P. Hazel

Library of Congress Control Number: 2012901726
ISBN: Hardcover   978-1-4633-2007-2
                    Softcover   978-1-4633-2009-6
                    Ebook   978-1-4633-2008-9

To order additional copies of this book, contact:
Palibrio
1663 Liberty Drive, Suite 200
Bloomington, IN 47403
Tel: 877.407.5847
Fax: +1.812.355.1576
orders@palibrio.com
385248

CONTENTS

DEDICATED TO:

- All of those who support freedom of speech and fight against racism and discrimination around the world.

- Those who have been murdered because their believes on the Human Rights as the most valuable principle.

-My family that I left alive and now are dead and I was unable to assist to their funerals.

-My family who I brought with me and stay close with their support.

The Author

UNEXPECTED ENCOUNTER

Meisa was a woman who had emigrated from a neighbouring country at the age of twenty-six years. She came from a family that was strictly Christian and she dedicated her life to the church, providing domestic services to a small parish church, at the head of which, was her uncle (the priest). Her brothers, eleven in total, worked in agriculture and ensured the prosperity of the familial properties. She was raised among men who used to paid little attention to the troubles of a woman, given their cultural traditions.

But changes began when Meisa's mother became gravely ill—Meisa took on all the responsibilities of her care until her final moments. Almost at the end, she was asked by her mother to take care of the household even she was the second amongst her brothers, but being the only female, her responsibility was to take her mother's place at home. Once the days of anguish had passed, her brothers agreed that she would now take over the role of their mother in the household, a role which had provided her with the only source of advice and counsel in the past. The responsibilities and the memories terrorized Meisa, and she sought guidance from the family priest who suggested to her the possibility of finding a different social environment. It did not take her long to make a decision and she took immediate action by stating to her brothers that she renounced all possible inheritance that belonged to her, and that she had decided to travel with the priest, who had been transferred to another parish in a country which, according to the evaluation or classification made by international experts, was included in the "third world" group. It had magnificent natural resources: coffee plantations, sugar cane, tobacco, cotton and other consumer products—all things that determine the status of wealth in an economic system. Unfortunately, only those born in wealth and the owners of lands benefited from any financial gain. They ignored the fact that the ones who deserved even the most minimal reward for their efforts were those workers who for hours and hours dedicated their lives to work the lands.

Meisa and her uncle left by bus early in the morning. It was an exhausting journey. Meisa was abandoning what represented financial comfort for her, but which at the same time limited the possibilities of having a future that she should find acceptable.

It took two days to get to her new home. Everything was different—the people, the buildings, the shopping areas.

Upon taking possession of his new church, the priest decided to hire her on as the main keeper of the temple to take care of all domestic duties in order to serve the religious community, he also offered temporary accommodation while she familiarized herself with the new setting.

Meisa did not go out except to fulfill necessary errands and had little contact with the community, save for ceremonies or special events. She used to go shopping for those who lived in the parish, on Sundays after her chores, at the main outdoor market in the area. That is how she began a new life at the age of twenty-six years in a new and unfamiliar country.

Also from an immigrant family was Whan, whose father had came to the same country from Europe, when the First World War had just started, at the young age of five years. His father had made and raised the family in a farm where the workers resided in a semi-feudal system. Whan was the second of six brothers and had the opportunity to attend the rural school, which he left after completing the third grade, which was customary for boys of that time.

He was nine years old when he started working to help the family—this of course was not a problem as this was expected and he was obliged to fulfill his responsibilities. His work consisted of proportionately helping the labourers that worked in agriculture and livestock. His duties began at five o'clock in the morning and ended at five o'clock in the afternoon. He lived in an environment where traditions, respect for others, and responsibilities were the basis for family relations. Whan was a youth dedicated to his activities—puberty was hidden between adolescence and adulthood. In his short life, he had developed a personality both robust and dominant.

On one particular occasion, Whan committed what was considered a grave fault. He was severely punished. He felt he was humiliated in front of his family and he locked himself in his room. At midnight of the same day, he left his home and his family—he was twelve years old. He travelled with no destination in mind until he decided to look for support from an uncle who lived roughly twenty kilometers away. That is where he stayed and learned to work with wood. Even though he felt no resentment toward his father, he did not visit him, even when he learned his mother had died. On weekends he would go to the downtown area of the city to purchase personal items, he would converse with friends in central park, and as it got late, he would return home.

Mondays were nothing more than the beginning of his weekly routine. Having had an inadvertent youth, he grew to be an adult who was interested in no more than survival. During one of his trips to the city, he met Meisa, who coincidentally frequented the same locales. In spite of the timidity and lack of social interactions under which Whan had been raised, and the muteness and mistrust practiced by Meisa with male companions, they managed to start a friendship that grew comfortable over months, and eventually became romantic. Whan was thirty years old and Meisa twenty-eight when they decided to become a couple. Meisa carried out her duties at the parish as usual while Whan continued with his own activities at the ranch house.

Months later they decided to rent a room where they lodged temporarily. Whan worried about finding a job that would allow for improvement in their financial situation; because of his tenacity and dedication, he was hired as a labourer by a well-known store in the city; his work consisted of loading and unloading merchandise from trucks. His low level of education did not prove to be a barrier when his duties were being assigned; these included controlling inventory of goods (incoming and outgoing) manually, calculating value of goods, reconciliations, and other similar tasks.

This job became vital in changing their economic status and in a short time they were able to relocate to an area at the north side of the city. This meant that Meisa would have to leave her work at the parish and throw herself entirely, as was the tradition in Latin American countries, into caring for their home. They started a new life with many changes to their normal routine while having all the necessities for a comfortable home.

The new community had all necessary resources for recreation and other activities for its residents: a movie theater, an elementary school up to sixth grade, a small food court, garages for the repair and maintenance of vehicles, establishments that made available all primary goods required in a home, and an office for printing and officiating documents. The neighbours all knew each other well and were united due to the proximity, their day-to-day issues of life, and their common needs. There were also five or six families in the area that were financially stable—they owned some of the businesses in the neighbourhood. However, socially, separate levels of status did not exist—but there was one thing missing from the small community—a church. The residents showed little interest in spiritualism without ever indicating an inclination for lack of morals. They lived a routine life in accordance with cultural and traditional values: husbands or partners worked hard jobs, children studied during school or played soccer in any area that was available. According to the usage, once the boys looked physically able or sixteen years of age, they should be ready and willing to join the army. Many times they had run away from the soldiers who tried to catch and enroll them by force. Mothers were responsible for everything that had to do with home chores and its activities.

Meisa's arrival and her dedication to the spiritual generated a small change in the community. With her restless Christian Catholic beliefs she visited different families with the objective of awakening in them the need of a place where they could unite and pray. She had varied results and even though there were only a small number of families that supported her, it was enough to get the project underway.

In the little time she had lived in the neighbourhood, Meisa had found a small, unoccupied property that youngsters used for sporting activities on weekends. She and two neighbours visited the owner and made a formal petition that involved giving up part of the location on a loan for the construction of a small Catholic parish. In order to satisfy the residents the owner agreed, not on loan but as a donation in the name of the community with the condition that the residents themselves would develop the necessary documents to present to the municipal authorities and that a committee would be formed and organized before formal possession.

The committee was formed with the help of the residents. Christian signs began to rise and after a short time the community became more participative in religious issues; one of the Members was Meisa, who with her own initiative, participated in all activities required in the construction of the small temple. They asked for authorization from the Archbishopric for the development of what would be a spiritual arena. Previously, anyone wanting to attend church or who just wanted to talk to a priest had to travel five kilometers, which was a problem for children and the elderly—with a parish in the community, this problem would be solved.

The project was realized with the voluntary help of the neighbours—the result was a small chapel called San Benito in honour of an Italian frail in Palermo who had been an example of virtues and sacrifices for humanity. Unfortunately, and of course naturally, there were those whose negativity towards the spiritual were led to commit criminal acts such as breaking into the church (taking advantage of the darkness of the night) and stealing the art work that had been acquired with funds collected from the neighbours. This made it necessary for someone to be hired (someone from the community) to watch and protect the church and its belongings. The committee decided to construct a house adjacent to the church—this house was offered to Meisa and Whan—they would live in this house and in return, they would protect the church and everything in it. All preparations for celebrations and special events would be their responsibility.

The couple took the offer of the committee and agreed to be responsible for the church, just as was required by the Archbishop to conserve the respect and values of the religion. Meisa conducted doctrine on Saturday afternoons; Sunday morning masses were held under the tutelage of whatever priest had been assigned on that particular day.

Meisa and Whan gained popularity in the community for the activities they took on for the church and for the taking on the responsibility and administration of eclectic resources. With everything that was happening, they did not forget their personal life and they had their first child two years later. The new routine did not make any changes, save for those that come with the movement of nature. Both met their social obligations and attended to the needs of the home.

A Different Childhood

Amilkar was the third of five children including the oldest sister. Sadly, the youngest of the five died at the age of two years from an illness that could have been treated, had Meisa's and Whan's financial situation been different.

Amilkar began to show abilities for learning at a very young age. Due to a mother who was completely dedicated to the Christian faith, the children helped in church every Sunday. Their father did not—he did not have as much passion for the religion as Meisa, but he never tried to oppose her beliefs. Even so, he complied with all his responsibilities by protecting the church, while also working full-time during the week.

At three years old, Amilkar could recite all basic prayers in Christian doctrine from memory. This was one of the first forms of evidence that attested to his intellectual abilities. He was challenged with doctrinal competencies organized by the church and he performed with ease. By the age of five and with an incredible precocity, he directed the evening Rosary. With the help of his older sister, he learned the letters of the alphabet and numbers using a book that was popular for children at the time—El Silabario (The Syllabus). At his young age he could read, write, and express ideas; this was all very uncommon for children of his age. He participated with Meisa in the doctrine lectures on Saturdays and would read excerpts from the sacred book, actions that surprised those in attendance. His initial inclination seemed to be oriented entirely towards religious means and not to social or cultural life.

He impressed many but he still did not meet the requirements for structured education as he was too young (the minimum requirement was for the child to be seven years of age by the month of February). While other children played in the street, Amilkar was at church reading children's books, improving his knowledge on his own. On some occasions, Whan took him to work as a distraction and Amilkar used the time to play with the construction materials the he was allowed—he would count nails and other small tools and would then organize them and store them in their proper slots. This also facilitated learning as he was using numerical skills hands-on in a practical setting.

At six years old, his mother, motivated by her son's wishes to attend school, took him to meet the principal of the community school. Her application was rejected but upon reading some of the supporting references regarding the child's abilities, the principal grew curious and he decided to give him a test. The results left him surprised and he immediately admitted Amilkar into grade one in elementary school.

This was a great change for the youngster. School as an educational structure represented not only entertainment, but also a moral responsibility, as he explained many years later. The school year was from February until October and in the three months of vacation, he visited the nearest church on a daily basis, where he learned the duties of an Acolyte or assistant of a parish in liturgical celebrations. He learned the Latin rituals and further expanded his knowledge of ecclesiastical procedures.

He had no difficulties with the learning process in school. He was fascinated by knowledge. He enjoyed adult books and put aside those written for children of his age. In the first few years of school he continually resulted at the head of his class as he paid full attention and dedication to his teachers. Silent when necessary, expressive when it was required—this was his way of learning. He competed in a friendly manner with four classmates during tests—they alternated "first place" and during the first four years of elementary education, Amilkar was awarded certificates of achievement and diplomas recognizing his exemplary behavior.

Amilkar's abilities had not gone unrecognized by the principal. Upon completing grade 4, the principal approached Meisa and commented to her that it might be possible for a transfer to a private school in the Catholic system, administered by priests of the Silesian order. This was an institution for students with financially "well-off" families and it had access to educational resources that allowed for the student to have a better idea of the teaching-learning phenomenon and process. The school was also known for physically stimulating over-achieving students with trips to recreational centres at no cost to the students. All of these factors were points of attraction for fathers and they worked and saved part of their income for up to three years for the fees.

However, according to schooling regulations, a student had to attend the school in their given area of residence, therefore it was going to be difficult to achieve the transfer. Also, the school required a monthly payment per student and Meisa had many limitations in this area. In spite of all the barriers, Amilkar was taken to the Headmaster of the school. This man was very interested in the child and he researched all of his qualifications: recommendations, school marks, conduct, and also the necessary documents to begin the process of a transfer. He contacted the proper authorities and presented Meisa's situation including her moral values and religious background—in a short time, authorization was granted for Amilkar to be admitted to the school. However, the financial problem was still present. The principal met with the association of fathers of the families and explained the situation and also highlighted Amilkar's educational achievements, which resulted in a scholarship being made available—all payments from Meisa were exonerated for the entirety of Amilkar's time at the school.

Amilkar's scholarly problem was resolved. The school was about five kilometers away from his home. At the age of ten and admitted to grade five of elementary education he embarked on yet another new experience, this time in a completely different environment. He was leaving behind his friends and classmates, whom more than likely he would never see again.

The first few days were difficult—because of the distance to the school and he had to walk, he had to get up much earlier than normal if he wanted to make it in time for the first prayings. The daily schedule consisted of two parts: morning from 7am to 11:30am and afternoon from 1pm to 4:30pm. He performed the same walking routine per day and on Sundays he helped with religious services at the church—this was part of the educational curriculum. With the passing of the months he became completely used to his new routine. His new classmates were not very communicative but Amilkar understood the situation. As the school had a religious character, there were frequent times of prayer and oration throughout each day and he participated in these with enthusiasm; this helped him to build friendships with his classmates. He was selected to sing in the school choir, though he had never practiced singing before. His participation in cultural and religious activities at school became more frequent, and he also joined in different sports as was suggested to him, without ever becoming a "star".

He never turned down a new request even if he had no knowledge of the task as he felt that accepting every assignment was the way to show his gratefulness at the kindness he was shown in being admitted to the school. He remembers two of his greatest moments in his first school year: the first was when he was selected to carry a flag at the parade held during patriotic festivities; the other when he and the choir performed at the year-end ceremony at a local theater a piece from Aida by Giuseppe Verdi.

Once the first school year ended, the principal talked with Meisa regarding Amilkar's religious inclinations, which he felt were strong and so, he suggested that Amilkar be included in an intensive three-month program, the three vacation months that included Christmas and the New Year, in which he would be recognized as a student aspiring towards the Seminary to begin a career in priesthood.

Meisa took this information as a special message. For her, this was significant enough to be a dream, but she had to discuss it with Amilkar, though she was sure he would accept as she felt confident she knew his feelings towards the church. As she had hoped, the youngster accepted without objection. At ten years old, school and participating in important activities provided him with confidence in his decisions.

The program for preparation into priesthood began in the beginning of October. The group was made up of 7 candidates, including Amilkar, all of similar ages and with the same long-term aspirations. He had to be at the school from 7am until 6pm every day of the week for lectures, lessons, and everything else necessary. At night, he helped his mother with the sacred Rosary. Saturdays the group of candidates went on trips for recreational breaks. Sundays in the afternoons were his only moments with his family. It was an intensive preparation that could be exhausting to someone of Amilkar's age, but he was able to value and respect his mother's efforts. At the end of the three months evaluations began to select those who would qualify for junior seminary. From the group, only one did not qualify, the rest met all the requirements of the program and were sent to different junior seminaries throughout the country.

Amilkar and Meisa received the news with great appreciation. His attendance at junior seminary was scheduled for January 6th. He would celebrate Christmas and the New Year with his family and this event resulted in being one of the saddest of his life. Traditionally, Meisa organized the "posada"—a night watch in some sense, of the sacred couple, Mary and Joseph—she was helped by neighbours and they took turns maintaining the watch. With her children, she would arrange the Nativity Scene in a corner of the house. Christmas celebration was always, as was traditional for humble families, on December 24th with a special dinner, explosions of firecrackers with friends, and the wait for a present which sometimes never arrived. She and her family attended Midnight Mass and then they waited for the New Year. On December 31st there were more special celebrations—family dinner and exploding firecrackers at midnight. That night, Amilkar remembers going to his room and being unable to contain his tears. In one week he would leave everything that surrounded him: his family, his friends, his schoolmates. It was not a permanent separation, only a temporary sacrifice that would last years. His life seemed to be on a fast-track, pressurized course. The academic and religious studies gave him much experience at his young age; it seemed a premature maturity.

Experiences at
Junior Seminary

———

He started at junior seminary in January when he was near eleven years of age. He would prepare for a career that was not very popular, that lacked social status and which was in no way luxurious when practiced with the necessary dedication and with ecclesiastical objectives; this was explained to him during the three months of preparation: a true priest is one that protects the humble and guides spiritually, one whose wealth is comprised of words that carry as a virtue, humility, and whose only instrument is faith. That is what he was taught and he hoped to comply with the responsibilities that represented the basis of a spiritual guide.

The integral process of a priesthood career required twelve years: five years in junior seminary and seven in senior seminary. In the first five years, regular academic courses were studied for official education with aggregates specific to religious work. These consisted of Biblical Lecture and Interpretation, Introductory and Intermediate Latin, and Principles or Canons of the Catholic Church. The next four years were spent in senior seminary and were dedicated to the study of Religious Philosophy; for certain students, these years were the most difficult, both due to the content and to the spiritual repercussions. It was the essence in developing the personality of a priest.

Picture # 1.

Two new seminarians when Amilkar was in his second year

Between the stages of Philosophy and Theology, one year was granted for practical experience. This consisted of the students being sent to different social institutions or parishes where they could familiarize themselves with direct work. Afterwards they would return to the seminary to finish three years of Theology. When the superiors considered a student to be prudent and after analyzing his qualities, the candidate should receive orders as a "Sub-Deacon", whose role inside of the Catholic Church is to assist the Deacon, and his position is above the lecturer in the catholic hierarchy church; after a short period, usually six months, he should be able to receive the "Deacon" order. This is one of the most important positions of the Catholic Church. His responsibilities and functions are close to the priest and is able to substitute him in emergencies, but in the whole celebration of special rites. Finally, the "Presbyterate" order is given. As a Minister, a priest is responsible for leading the spiritual side of his parish, a community assigned by the geographical distribution of the followers. It is an order which last for the rest of the priest life, even if he stops performing his duties. All of this was done in a frenzy of religious discipline and total relinquishment to others.

The seminary work was arduous as soon as the period of what represented "imprisonment" began; the activities and occupations were greatly varied and they started at 5am; normal responsibilities of cleaning were expanded with studies, homework, and philosophical and theological orientations. Once a week they went out for brief trips of distraction—they walked a few kilometers enjoying the outdoors, then, they would return to continue with the pending activities of the day. Visits with family were limited to once or twice per month. In spite of the intense studies and daily work, Amilkar lived in an environment of peace and tranquility. The intense routine was never an obstacle. He visited his family once per year for three days (generally before Christmas) and always returned to the seminary.

His intelligence and dedication to studying facilitated a quick adaptation to the spiritual lifestyle. He was an over-achieving student. Again, he was a member of the seminary choir, he participated in theatrical works, and he learned basic usage of musical instruments, all of which represented a distraction outside of his spiritual tasks without ignoring the significance of priestly services. He always went above and beyond the expectations of a spiritual guide. This was his life for five years.

He was in the fifth and last year of junior seminary; he was preparing to enroll in senior seminary for the next year, but something unexpected changed Amilkar's dreams and aspirations: an earthquake of great intensity had destroyed the city where his family lived, directly affecting the community where he was born and raised. It was a moment of sadness and uncertainty. He asked for permission to visit his family and this was granted immediately. He felt something completely unknown to him that he could not explain and he said good-bye to his seminary mates, putting his return in doubt. He did not have any misgivings about his religious vocation but his thoughts were fully turned on his family. This was a dilemma: he had left his family to follow priesthood and religious doctrine but he felt that in dire circumstances he should be with those who needed him.

He left in the late hours, as the sun began to descend. The trip would take approximately two hours by train. He speculated on what he would find at home and doted on what he was leaving behind. He asked himself if he had made the right decision. The seminary had taken five years of his life and these represented for him an experience that was fundamental for his future. His worry about the well-being of others led him to his home in these moments of chaos, he told himself, as if trying to justify the decision he had made. At the same time he wondered if this was no more than an excuse to leave his religious career. He was now seventeen years old. He was an adolescent with such preparation and maturity that he could face any situation that awaited him.

COMMUNITY ENCOUNTER

He arrived in the city, he left the train behind and halfway to his neighbourhood, he saw scenes of hopelessness. Buildings collapsed to the ground, houses completely destroyed. Stores fashioned of tarp and homes of sheetmetal or cardboard now stood where before had been a structure that covered minimal necessities for the locals. There was constant rain which served only to make conditions more miserable.

Finally he reached what had once been his house; it was semi-destroyed and the property that had been used for religious activities was now practically inundated by the residents that had lost their homes. They had found temporary refuge here—there were new small rooms built with the help of the government and social organizations.

Amilkar's arrival surprised his family. It was a visit they never would have expected. Meisa gave him a long and hard hug but she was still preoccupied—she wondered what the reason was behind her son's presence. Whan, his father, was hospitalized. He was working as a Night Watchman and had been held-up at gunpoint—he was shot in the leg. He was unable to provide any laborious help at this point. Amilkar let his family know that he was there because he was worried about them, wanted to know what was happening directly, and was offering help.

The conditions he found in his neighbourhood were not even close to satisfactory. Morality was at an all-time low. The sudden arrest of productive and industrious activities, and other laborious tasks had caused all companies to halt work—the result was that people found entertainment that was less than savoury. Prices on basic necessities had reached untouchable heights for the humble and the few programs the government had implemented of humanitarian aid for those in need were being abused by those responsible for distributing the goods—because of this, these programs were suspended and the only people affected were the victims of the disaster.

Amilkar tried to re-incorporate municipal assistance by making contact with the authorities—they in turn offered the services once again, this time doing a direct distribution to the community using transport vehicles that belonged to the state. Amilkar volunteered to organize this project. The residents misused the assistance again and asked for financial assistance instead; when this did not work they started selling the goods that were being donated to them. The government suspended the program again.

Picture # 2.
Community condition after the earthquake

In their defense, the residents had lost their religious values at this point; the priest responsible for the church felt that those habituating the religious terrain did not deserve to be there as they were participating in malicious and immoral activities on a daily basis. However, he did not wish to abandon the people and so he asked Amilkar for help, as assistant of social activities for the neighbours.

Amilkar accepted and immediately began to research information and compile documents to find possible solutions. He planned and implemented a survey and he presented the results to municipal authorities. It took approximately one year for the municipality to make the first offer of assistance to the community. This consisted of placing them in a locale that had once been acquired by a move of the armed forces but that as of yet, had not been habituated. The accommodations would be constructed by the municipal government at low cost to the people. Amilkar communicated the proposal to the residents and it was accepted. They began to leave their refuge, leaving behind filth and trash. The municipality offered their services to clean the property. Once ready, the parisher blessed the terrain again to cleanse the aggravations that the people had committed over the last two years.

The property with the parish was now ready to realize a project Amilkar had proposed in the past to the priest: the construction of a Catholic temple with a capacity proportionate to the density of the zone and that would be physically deserving of religious services. Financial assistance was sought from a humanitarian organization that happily accepted the petition and in a few months construction of the new temple started under Whan direction. A year later, the church San Benito was inaugurated and blessed. Meisa and Whan continued with the responsibilities of maintaining it, cleaning it and any other task that was necessary for religious occasions.

National University, a Second Option

Amilkar had been out of the seminary for approximately 2 years. Recent events had kept him incredibly occupied and he had not had any time to think about his circumstances. During this time however, he had gained insight and even a little experience in public administration. He had made contact with members of different political institutions and the bureaucracy under which, public resources were administered left him completely unsatisfied. He felt that the people needed to be heard, and not only in dire circumstances like the recent situation.

At nineteen years old he decided to look into the possibility of doing post-secondary studies at the National University, the only university that was an option at the time. The opinions surrounding the institution were divided; on the one side was the government, accusing students of communist beliefs and of conspiring against governmental stability; on the other side were the people, a population made up of labourers and humility, farmers, teachers, all aware of the fact that their needs were not being met even in the lowest of standards, a group that found in the university an ally that would help them improve their sad conditions and pauper-like way of living.

When Amilkar shared his plans with his family, Meisa opposed him completely. She felt fear at the possibility of her son losing his religious inclinations. She was influenced by governmental propaganda as well, and so was Whan. Despite his mother's objections, he did not change his mind—he was convinced and he signed up to do an entrance exam. It was not difficult for him; he was a student very used to discipline and his educational background superseded that of the other students. In a few months he received a letter of acceptance. He also applied for a scholarship which would relieve him of monthly payments if he kept his grades above the requirement imposed by the university. This application was also accepted. In this way he gave himself to another temple of studies, much different from the one he had grown to know.

In those years, the National University required all students to take basic studies, known as Common Areas, in which students had the opportunity to gain general academic knowledge and then make an informed decision regarding a long-term profession in accordance with their skills and abilities. This lasted 2 years but this academic preparation made it possible for Amilkar to choose a career in six months; he registered in the faculty of Economics and studies began immediately.

He entered into a different world. The university allowed for flexibility of studies, having students choose their own courses, all of which were in accordance with their university degree plan which was designed by university authorities. It was the complete opposite of his previous life; a reserved and mystic way of life in the seminary where everything was dictated without options or opinions. He viewed the university's reputation with suspicion. It was said that the university was Marxist and that it followed communist ways, on top of being an enemy to anything that was associated with religion. His first experiences were of becoming familiar with the student environment where everything was significant of free participation. He expressed ideas and opinions openly without fear of being opposed. He took full responsibility of his words with a confidence that in most cases was subjected to the polemic influences of religious philosophies that he knew extremely well, while respectfully listening to the materialistic leniencies of his classmates.

The self-discipline he had learned in the seminary helped him to effectively plan and organize his time. His first semester in university was a period of adaptation. His previous studies had been in small class sizes and groups (in junior seminary, the members were selected and annually accepted in no more than groups of two or three), while the university, in the first couple of years had up to four hundred students in one class. Being who he was, he always looked in be in the front of his classes. He was obsessed with his studies. The courses he was required to take included (among others) General Sociology based on historic materialism, General Philosophy, Economics and of course, Math and Statistics. The first three were exactly what Amilkar had hoped for. They focused on the reality of human nature and its unsatisfied needs, being limited by productive and authoritative factors whereby activities and movements progressed in such a way to benefit only those individuals in power.

The distribution of goods was criticized with reason and equality was fought for, an equality that signified a betterment of the conditions of quality of life for the general public. Humanity should never sit and wait for the hand of God to resolve life issues, it is the responsibility of the human being to understand that we all have the same rights when it comes to satisfying our needs, it was said. It was stated that a reorganization and redistribution of productive factors/sources could be an option in order to dissolve the poverty of the majority of classes, but neither the state nor those in privileged classes made any move in this direction.

In spite of the fact that the involvement of the church either in favour of or opposed to the system was never directly criticized, indirectly it was considered that the church's silence in the face of political phenomena represented a sort of approval of the system. Amilkar's thoughts and criterion kept his vision of religion intact, but he began to realize that there was a great difference between the well-known significance of the church and of the spiritualism of the religion itself. He defined the church as a social structure with a hierarchy that limits the power of its members and that establishes the rules or commandments of the religion as the model of spiritual conduct expected of humanity. Religion, he emphasized, is used by many as an instrument to attract the innocence and ignorance of a weak community. Generally, the newly enlightened do not go to middle or upper classes—the targets are humble societies.

Church authorities define religion in their own terms and divide the church, confusing human beings. They spoke of being the leaders of a great organization that they call "church" leaving aside spiritual values, donning the belief in one God and orienting objectives towards commercial value. Amilkar was a firm critic of those who were self-proclaimed spiritual guides without having the most minimal, fundamental knowledge of the values of religion. They carry the bible under their armpit to attract the unintelligent he would say; they memorized biblical passages and modified them to suit their own interests. This generates a high level of competition that reaches up to the construction of temples, with the idea that those that use the most economic resources are the ones that offer greater truth.

When Amilkar was about to finish his first semester at the university, a greatly important phenomenon occurred in his life. In the areas that border the neighbouring country, that country where Meisa came from, worked hundreds of foreign labourers on the side where she actually lived—these workers collaborated with the economic development of the area. They had spent many years dedicating their time and labour to these activities; the recent elections in the country had resulted in a president that did not see this labour as beneficial and he decided to replace the foreign workers and sent them away with nothing, obligating them to abandon the only life they knew and all the work they had produced over so many years. Some of them were second generation workers, born in the country, but this made no difference to government officials.

Coincidentally, the dates for the elimination rounds of the World Cup of Soccer had been set in that same month, both countries being considered strong candidates to make the cut. The expulsion of the agricultural workers was already under way through communications between the two countries under the leadership of the officials, and this angered the people of both countries. Therefore, when members of the two soccer teams and their fans went to the neighbouring country, they were mistreated by the locals on both ends.

The military government in Amilkar's country responded by declaring war without reason. In approximately four days this government invaded the neighbouring territory, murdered innocents, burned down houses and robbed the little possessions that the labourers had gained through a long life of hard work.

Innocently, students from the university had organized groups that would travel to the border by bus to help soldiers and other citizens that had been hurt in combat; among these students was Amilkar who had offered his services without reserve. Everything came to a halt. At the moment of departure they were informed that the war was nothing more than a ploy developed by the military governments of both countries to develop new work projects for which the labourers were not needed. These workers lived on these lands and the only way to get rid of them was to fill them with terror via a war—in this way they would evacuate the area and leave the land available for the government to take.

The student groups were disbanded but the actions of the military began to have serious consequences. Many of the citizens of the neighbouring country who had lived in this new country for years and who had made this new country their second home began to be attacked. Everything that bore the name of the neighbour country was suspended: streets, buildings, monuments and schools. Meisa received anonymous letters at church—at a particular community event, she mentioned to those in attendance that she had received threatening letters and to her surprise, they gave her all of their support and urged her to stay in the country. She felt comfortable and safe and so offered to stay and continue her church services.

International reporters were not given access to the areas of combat and so used sport as the excuse for the war. They offered the world the news as "The Soccer War". Even to this day, it is unknown if this was their own idea or if the military governments had a hand in the media coverage.

Each of these occurrences made an impact on Amilkar's way of thinking, someone who leaned mostly towards helping others. Spiritualism, he expressed in one occasion, has no significance if humanity does not have the material elements for survival.

THE POSSESSION OF THE NATIONAL UNIVERSITY

Amilkar was about to finish his third year at the university when the institution was overtaken by the military. Students were murdered, important documents were burned, and the labs and popular clinic of the faculty of medicine were destroyed. The damage targeted at all the facilities, in all the faculties of the university was, and still is, one of the most cruel acts aimed directly at intellect on the part of the ignorance of authorities, led by an elite group that validated itself with the power of arms in the hands of criminals, attempting to transform the liberal and democratic thinking of students by implementing an educational regimen developed to benefit the interests of the privileged classes.

The facilities were unavailable for use for two years. The university was suspended by government authorities. It was a desperate measure taken by the authorities to silence the voices and opinions of the students. Amilkar experienced for the second time a movement of physical force aimed at the physical impotence of the people.

This action led to an infinite number of private universities being opened; they were made possible through high, monthly fees with almost no pre-requisites, and admitted students that did not want to lose their professional careers. The commercialization of higher level education became part of the educational system. In a period of approximately two years, dozens of universities covered the educational market; some of them without legal authorization but this was not seen as an obstacle since the Ministry of Education considered these universities to be assisting the system and therefore turned a blind eye, with the hope that people would forget what happened to the National University which, according to educational authorities, was the location housing socialists that were organizing with the goal of destabilizing the government; this was merely a cowardly course taken to hide the actions of the military who, in order to protect those in power, committed a travesty against the superior temple of education.

Amilkar did not see these new private universities as institutions that would permit him to fulfill his dreams and goals. He considered that they only existed to serve their own purposes and waited patiently for the re-opening of the National University, an action which was continually pushed back, creating doubt and disquiet within the student community with low financial resources.

In one of his meditating moments he remembered the words of the head priest at the seminary, words he expressed upon Amilkar's departure: "The teacher, like the priest, has also the yen to serve and to help those around him with no need of dressing in habit, and the first teacher after all, was Jesus Christ".

Amilkar's Entry to the Teaching Profession

In that same era, the educational system of all academic levels was being reviewed and an educational Reform was being planned. One of the objectives was to diversify secondary education in order to provide options to the student and that in this way, the student could focus on an educational field of choice where his or her abilities would allow for mastering an area in a shorter period of time than that required by universities and that as a semi-professional, could be integrated into the labour force.

These revisions to the system involved the necessity for qualified professionals which were lacking in educational authorities and organizations. The educators that worked in schools and other public institutions had been trained in the traditional school system, and even though their moral and academic background was exemplary, they were unfamiliar with the technicalities in areas such as health, economics, tourism and agriculture, which were all new projects making up secondary education. Even so, public authorities hired traditional educators that did not have knowledge of the new course content with the sole intent to fill a vacancy without considering the learning need of the students. The same situation existed in the private institutions that hired personnel with no credentials in regards to technical knowledge, in this way justifying low salaries; consequently the quality of academics required from students was lacking on a national level and employers, both private and public, abstained from hiring these individuals, increasing unemployment rates. Because of the need for an income, new grads were forced to work in areas completely unrelated to their educational background, such as being messengers, collections officers (on motorcycles) and vendors.

The favoured sector was the Organization of Private Catholic Colleges. These institutions depended on economic possibilities to hire professionals in the proper fields, while at the same time increasing monthly payments to students. The student mass of these colleges was made up of descendants and family relatives of the higher class which was significant as these educational institutions held political thoughts and philosophies that were a continuation of that which belonged to those already in power. However, this situation opened the doors for National University students of advanced academic levels to become involved in the educational process, providing services to private institutions without the requirement of having a degree in Education.

Amilkar considered the preparation and training he had acquired at the university in the commercial field and decided to solicit employment at a private institution as a professor of Economic Sciences, Marketing, and Business Administration. After a grueling interview he was hired and he began a career as a post-secondary professor. He had the necessary academic resources backing him and he felt confident about his competencies in regards to educating students in spite of the fact that he did not have a degree to certify him as a teacher. He was twenty-two years old when he started his educational work.

In the first three years of working as a professor, he devoted the greater part of his time to research and collecting information while he instructed in the classroom. His first step was to organize his notes from university and develop a booklet that his students used as a class text. The cost of the books suggested by the Ministry of Education was not in accordance with the economic levels of the students in the middle class, therefore students and professors at other institutions were constantly requesting copies of his booklets for instructional material. In this way he began to gain popularity among teachers and students.

From the daily contact with young students he became aware of inappropriate attitudes and conducts that generated reactions of the same nature from teachers and principals who solved issues with punishment, from very lenient acts to actually expelling students from school. They attributed this behaviour to lack of discipline or to non-compliance to internal rules belonging to a regiment that gave institutions the right to selective admission of students. Amilkar felt that public and private educational centres lacked psychological supports, and he voluntarily provided emotional assistance and guidance making good use of his studies in Psychology and Sociology and of the moral values he acquired at the seminary.

Issues presented themselves immediately. Rebellion, disciplinary acts and the little interest that most students showed in their studies were only the results of the minimal nutrition, fragile matrimonial relations, limited family income and the disinterest combined with a lack of skills in technical-professional fields. Amilkar contributed by having discussions with the family members of the students, and he listened and counselled the students themselves when the opportunity presented itself. His work was misinterpreted by some principals that believed that this social service was actually a political intervention that was not part of educational curricula. Because of this his services were suspended by all the principals at the private institutions in which he worked. In spite of everything, his work in the classroom as a specialist in economic sciences was not meddled with.

The Ministry of Education considered his experience and his knowledge to be of value and he was solicited as a professor to evaluate the results of private exams which consisted of a final test at the national level that students had to pass in order to obtain degrees in their respective fields. These tests were taken by students in public institutions, just the same as students in private centres. His work in the evaluation process impressed the educational authorities and he was offered the opportunity to provide his services at a public institution.

His experience allowed him to develop into an exemplary professional. He became a voluntary member of social, academic and athletic organizations and activities. He organized soccer competitions for staff members from different educational institutions, both public and private. The objective was to bring professors together and after games on weekends, they would discuss the phenomena of national life. The soccer competitions became known as the "Tournament of Magisterial Friendship". The competitions were done annually and every year, new institutions signed up to a part of it, elongating the ropes of friendship amongst professors.

Not everything was positive however. The central government was experiencing an economic crisis and the management of the budget was argued over by government officials and the opposition whose representatives saw nothing satisfactory in the solutions the government proposed.

The political system, which was already debilitated by open corruption, gave the opportunity for all of its activities to be doubted and to generate mistrust in the people.

Hard-working professors, educators that like Amilkar worked in education without having a degree approved by the Ministry of Education that would certify them in their fields, were undergoing serious problems with salaries just the same as the rest of the population in the middle and lower classes. Paycheques were late or backed up and the authorities were paying no heed to complaints; the teachers found it necessary to create a committee that was supported by the National Organization of Teachers, and this committee would negotiate possible solutions for the current issues. The staff members considered the academic and intellectual preparation Amilkar had and they selected him to be a part of their group. This was the first movement in which Amilkar took an active role. The first meeting concluded with no acceptable solutions. Government authorities argued that the budget did not have room for teachers' salaries, with the teachers' committee rebutting that the rationale was out of place as their positions would not have been created by the school principals or directors without first having been approved and included in the economic funds available to them. Despite all arguments, the delegates of the ministry maintained their positions.

A second meeting was scheduled, this time with the head of the ministry himself. This one would take place at the offices of the Ministry of Education two days before Christmas. The group of teachers presented themselves at the offices and to their surprise, found the doors to the ministry closed. The workers were celebrating Christmas and the beginning of the holidays and would not be back until the sixth of January. Amilkar was at the head of the group and when he asked to see the Minister, a security officer of the building threatened him, said he knew who he was and told him to watch his steps. The professors that were present, approximately two thousand in total, were angered at this behaviour and threatened to take those responsible to justice as this was a direct threat to one of its members.

A delegate of the Ministry came out to express his respect and apologies and asked the committee for a new meeting after Christmas—Amilkar, representing his colleagues, accepted.

On December 27th a new meeting between the committee of educators, representatives of the Ministry of Education and of the Ministry of Hacienda took place—the latter presented the agreement written up and signed by the central government, in which the payments to those educators that were affected were authorized, but also the process established by the law to pay out late salaries would have to be followed. This would take time. Amilkar and the committee offered their professional knowledge so that wages could be released before the New Year. Once the process was finalized and wages were available, the agreement and decree had to be signed. The Delegate of the Ministry of Education signed and asked Amilkar to sign as representative of the teachers who would be paid on the 30th of December. That signature, which at that moment was being used to solve the issues educators were facing, would be used in the future as a permanent and discreet security measure by military against Amilkar.

In the face of previous misunderstandings and to avoid future confusion, the Ministry of Education decreed that post-secondary institutions, whether public or private, would not accept applications from teachers that did not have teaching degrees. The document would have to be authorized by the only existing official institution known as "Normal School for Educators" or by any university that followed the same educative plan. Of course, the primary objective of this decision was to eliminate the university students that, like Amilkar, lacked the degree, yet still worked as educators.

However, the need for teachers like Amilkar was evident. Approximately 75% of educators specialized in undergraduate studies and in the private sector fell in this category. The principals of educational centres that would be greatly affected inquired of the ministry to reconsider the decree.

The Ministry considered the petition and agreed to accept teachers under two conditions: those that decided to continue working in education had to have at least five years of experience in Education; the other that they continue their studies for two years and take appropriate courses including Pedagogy, Didactic, Psychology of Education, Educative Sociology, Evaluation Methods and Statistics.

This was not a problem for Amilkar. He registered in the courses—his experience in the seminary and his years as a university student as well as his time as an educator facilitated his path to an educational career. In a period of six months, he obtained his degree as an educator.

First Arrest and Threat on his Life

In this manner Amilkar continued his educational work in public and private institutions. He won the friendship and respect of his colleagues and heads of families due to his "charisma", as was stated by an old friend and professor. His work did not remain in a classroom—it projected to the moral aspect of life without ignoring the reality that occurred outside the walls of educational institutions. He helped his students with personal problems, organized recreational activities and joined them on social outings.

While this went on at the schools he was being observed by those that confused his relationship with his students and on many occasions they described him as a "dangerous type", to use the words of the para-military. He was stopped for the first time on his way to the bus stop that would take him to his home, the same route he took every day. His home was approximately twelve kilometers from his workplace; he was interrogated on the spot for nearly two hours and according to witnesses, it was a miracle that he was allowed to go. At that time it was well-known that any citizen who was stopped in the same way was either killed on the spot or ended up disappearing. Amilkar never discussed the content of the interrogation with anyone, but he was warned that sudden and physical action would be taken against him if necessary.

With his teaching degree he was automatically a member of the National Society of Educators, an intellectual force that was feared by the military. On a particular occasion, a high-ranking member of the military expressed his belief to Amilkar that a professor was a danger because "he is a thinker and he shares these thoughts with students, infecting their brains with lies", to which Amilkar responded that truth had no need of a deep analysis and that professors were not the ones responsible for student problems. It was enough to notice the level of malnutrition the people suffered, the lack of food resources in the homes, and the high rates of unemployed fathers who were fired for not agreeing with the abuses being practiced by employers, to see that the crisis students were in did not originate in the schools.

POLITICS IN THE TEACHING-LEARNING PROCESS

The conditions mentioned in the previous paragraph as causes of student conduct had roots in the political unrest of the internal system of the country. The people's dissatisfaction towards the government's impotency in regards to getting the country out of the socio-economic demise worsened day to day and employment organizations, agencies and other institutions were starting to use physical force against the armed forces of the political system. The government tried to gain international support by using effective means of communication to discredit the truths being expressed by popular organizations and with the help of the military, subjugated any citizen that independently, or through an organization manifested the need for change.

The central government with its internal problems was about to create chaos in political structures. There were leftist and rightist organizations that acted freely; the rightist ones enforced their power in the important cities of the country. They imposed their ways in spite of the complaints of the people who by means of unions and employment groups, proposed passive solutions. Presidential elections of that time were bloody. Elected governments were accused of meddling with the electoral process. The name of the president was new, but public administration was a continuation of the previous system, was adverse to the benefits of the people while looking out only for the interests of the privileged population, the elite class that had always controlled the country's economy and that directly or indirectly supported the actions of clandestine, military groups known as "squadrons of death" who arrested, kidnapped and killed anyone who did not conform to the rules and actions of those in power. They operated twenty-four hours a day and used violence to invade homes, killing families on the grounds that they were "suspected" of collaborating with the opposition. In the same manner they attacked cities and villages, they burned down entire communities while the government justified these acts by doting them "patriotic acts against the communists that wanted to take over the country". It was the most ridiculous idea a government had expressed on an international level.

The military gained more and more power, and with the help of the government of the United States of America, fought armed groups of the opposition and easily arrested any citizen with no investigation whatsoever.

The political differences between the government and the forces of opposition grew wider and wider with each passing day and it was the people, the general public that suffered the consequences. In the meantime, work authorities and business owners maintained firm in their decision to keep wages where they were.

THE PARTICIPATION
OF THE CHURCH

At this time the church was experiencing radical change. The Archbishop retired and left his post for a new individual to be chosen in his place. The church had kept itself outside the problems being faced by the people, save for a few short comments made in the weekly newsletter; their statements were not what faithful Christians hoped for and the neutral position held by the church became considered by the people as a sort of support for government actions. Even so, a change in religious orientations was still expected.

In a few short days the new Archbishop was named and this was released to the public. In his first public showing, the new Archbishop stated that he would continue to follow the current policies of the church according to the basis of Christianity. This disappointed many who had expected that with new religious leadership came a new sense of hope. Despite his statement, political complaints were made to the Archbishop. The church operated a small newspaper office in the centre of the city that ran on minimal business conditions and relied on donations to survive. The articles leaned towards the sentiments of the people and this was regarded as propaganda—this caused many attacks on the small office to the extent that it was burned down and the manager/editor was killed while walking down a busy street in broad daylight.

One of the most tragic events of the time was the murder of a priest and his assistant, a young boy—they were driving in their car to the parish house when they were ambushed by a group of soldiers. Violence had reached limits no one had dreamed of. The murder of a priest was seen as an extreme action taken by the military and government authorities did no more than "lament" the occurrence.

The event provoked many changes in the manner in which the political situation was being dealt with by the church, and the Archbishop began to make statements of opposition in mass towards any action taken against the church and its followers.

Years before at the Vatican, and in meetings of high church authorities in Puebla (Mexico) and Medellin (Colombia), it had been discussed that the church could participate to assist with the necessities of the lower classes that were continually oppressed in Latin America and internationally. However, the silence of the church in the face of the obvious violation of human rights in part of governments was criticized.

Due to the high number of complaints received at the offices of the Archbishop from labourers and humble citizens soliciting help to find numerous family members and friends that had "disappeared", an office was opened called "Legal Advice" which, supported by the International Commission of Human Rights, helped individuals with the legal process of officially searching for those that had gone missing. The participation of the church in human issues became highly necessary and it decided to adopt a more direct attitude in the city's disquiet and put a new principle into practice: "The Preferred Option for the Poor". The public was more involved in religious events and activities both in the cities and in small towns and villages. This new action taken by the church created nervousness in military leaders who in turn, decided to respond by increasing attacks on small communities that lacked protection.

However, communities also started to take action. Social groups of workers became political and they approached diverse political parties, looking for support and for their needs to be met; moderate leftist groups surged that supported discussions at a national level. There were also extreme leftists that held to the premise that it was impossible to discuss anything with civil authorities as the military openly disobeyed political constitutions in turning against its own people, and therefore the only solution was the use of arms. The country prepared for a battle riddled with arms and violence. Military groups used any excuse to arrest, beat and kill indiscriminately. They closed down main roads, held up public buses and it was enough to be a teacher, labourer or union worker to be arrested and murdered. Day after day corpses were found in all areas of the country.

Within military activities the utter disrespect for life came at a great cost. The time was unstable as war had not yet been declared and in a short time, five priests were murdered, three of them having been Amilkar's colleagues in junior seminary. The first died in a military invasion of a parish church in which a meeting of church authorities and youngsters was being held—the soldiers argued that they were looking for weapons and that those in the church had attacked them. In the end, no weapons were found, but the deed was done. A second priest was gunned down while walking through the central park of a city close to the capital—he was shot at from a hidden vehicle; the reason given by the head government and by the National Newspaper was that he was carrying money intended for guerilla groups. When an independent newspaper interviewed the Presbyterian assistant, he stated that the priest had 25 colones (about four dollars) that had been donated in mass and which he was depositing at the bank.

The same type of vehicle was used to kill a third priest who was hailed with bullets on a Sunday morning at the doors of his parish as he chatted with the attendees after mass. This time the government stayed silent. Nobody responded to these assassinations, yet everyone knew who the key players were. Only members of the military and their friends were authorized to drive that style of vehicle.

In all three cases, the ridiculous excuses made by the government created disgust in the general public and they looked to organizations as their only means of expressing indignation in response to the occurrences.

Relations between the government and the opposition became more tense and to discuss any possible solution became more distant little by little. The government and its actions was receiving criticism at an international level. Social and economic instability was imminent. Participation by the government of the United States was not held off—the president of the USA had approved millions of dollars and military forces to aid the country's government. The opposition saw these military members as "mercenaries" that argued their role was to protect the country from a communist invasion.

The government continued holding public activities and celebrations as though nothing were happening internally. In spite of everything, less and less people were attending these events, some due to a great fear of witnessing a massacre by the military and many to show their hatred towards authorities.

In a civic celebration, Amilkar was chosen by students and colleagues to give a speech to the attendees. He took this as an opportunity to mention to the people that violence was nothing more than the incapacity to think and that only those with brain damage used weapons to defend themselves from a ghost that some called Marxism—Leninism; to top it off, they were using the least recommendable instrument to attack it. He suggested that the principle could only be fought with another principle or idea, but their incapacity to develop an idea led them to kill without realizing that destroying a body does not destroy an idea.

He went on to comment on the murders of the priests, who other than being former fellow students, only cared for the salvation of souls by guiding human beings to a dignified path, something that their killers (murderers) considered a crime.

Amilkar's Second Arrest

That night Amilkar was walking to his parents' house when a taxi stopped in front of him. He was forced into the vehicle and the car moved to an unknown destination. There were witnesses on the street and these were forced to clear the area by a hail of bullets from one of the passengers.

They drove for little more than two kilometers—they limited themselves to telling him that his was a second warning and that there would not be a third. Amilkar asked them this: if they were members of the community, how could they kill their own? They did not respond and threw him out of the moving vehicle which continued on. Back on the street, Amilkar stood and followed the path the taxi had taken. He went back to the place where he was captured and those who had seen what happened were surprised to see him as they had given him up for dead. He managed to survive a second experience.

The next morning Amilkar was close to the institution where he taught in the mornings and he noticed a vehicle stopping right at the front doors of the building. Three men got out of the car and surprised a fellow teacher—they grabbed him forcibly from behind, back turned, and threw him on the ground. They proceeded to give him a severe beating, using hands and weapons. Amilkar ran at them but they immediately went back into the vehicle and left. The assaulted professor was taken to the hospital where he spent three days in intensive care. Two months later, this same professor was arrested, this time during the night. Amilkar was notified and he went to visit him in prison—he had been through a new round of torture. The commander on shift told Amilkar that the only way his friend would stay alive was if he left the country. The family sought out protection and they were sent to Australia. Another brain the country was wasting.

Amilkar went on with his educative work as always. In the morning he worked at a private college and in the afternoon, at an institution that was headed by an academic professor but that was administered by a coronel, as it was a special project of the armed forces. The staff was made up of civilians and received their salaries from government funds in the education branch, which provided them with a certain type of autonomy.

His morning work used to finish at 11:30am and afterwards he met up with a fellow professor with whom he had developed a close friendship as they shared ideals in regards to helping students and to anyone who needed it, which at that time was the large part of the population. They considered themselves politically neutral but they maintained the basic principles that human rights should be respected even if the cost is life itself.

They followed the same commuting route periodically. They boarded the bus that would take them downtown, got off at the same stop and from there, they would go their separate ways. On one of many occasions, Amilkar needed didactic materials and so, got off the bus one stop before the one he usually did. When he got to work the next day he was informed by the principal of the educative centre that his friend had been arrested at noon the day before. He was thrown violently into a black vehicle with tinted windows and no one knew where he was taken. A week later his friend's family told Amilkar that he was in a prison for political rebels and that he should not go visit as he was in danger of being arrested himself.

In this way many educators, teachers, professors and the like, were arrested or simply went missing, without going through court systems, or any legal processes. Without this privilege, many spent long periods of imprisonment with no chance of having visitors. Others had not had the same luck and had simply been killed. One morning as Amilkar opened the door of his house to go out, he found a dead body on his doorstep. It was a teacher that worked in a city close to the capital. He immediately reported this incident to the Teacher's Association as he considered this to be a direct message and threat from the criminals.

It was suggested by the directors of the Teacher's Association that Amilkar change residences and move to an area far from the city as a security measure, and he paid heed to this advice.

Since the number of violent acts happening around Amilkar only seemed to grow, his life and career looked very insecure. In spite of his neutral position, he had been captured twice, though he was free to go almost immediately.

The government's unwillingness to talk to the leaders of the rebel groups caused many strikes to occur among workers in the industry, which affected commerce and public development. Union representatives of workers for each industry had joined forces and became one organization known as The Syndicate Federation.

Specialized teacher's salaries were late once again. Months would pass and educational authorities did not show any motivation to solve the current situation. The Teacher's Organization developed a committee again to meet with the Ministry of Education; Amilkar was nominated as one of them and the response they received was that the fiscal year was about to end and that they would have to wait until the next year. This proposal was not accepted as there were teachers that did not have any other source of income; their families were in critical financial conditions. Unfortunately, this time there was no resolution to the problem—teachers had, more than likely, the worst Christmas of their lives, with no income and with many debts.

A new year began and things worsened due to the lack of interest shown by the government to provide solutions to the needs of the people, and to the unwavering position of the labour sector. Amilkar continued his educative work with the private and the state sectors, salaries continued to be undistributed, and the group of educators with which he was affiliated began to manifest ideas to initiate temporary pauses of work as the only means to push for productive talks and discussions. Union representatives and workers' associations of industry (construction and transport), as well as other institutions had opted for labour strikes.

The administrative deficiency degenerated governmental efficacy to the point of provoking a reaction from high military authorities which resulted in an internal revolution that eventually led to the deposition of the president of the republic. A junta made up of civilians and military officers was put in place—3 military members and 2 political representatives of the most popular parties. A legislative congress was erected temporarily and a provisional government cabinet was named, in which some members of the opposition were allowed to participate. From these new government officials, a new Minister of Education was named. His first act in government was to propose a project to the new government junta which consisted of increasing teachers' salaries by a hundred percent and to pay out all the backed up paycheques in a period of ten days. This proposal was approved immediately and within three days, all backed up wages were paid out in full. This went to show that was the negative attitude of the previous government was the true cause of salary issues and not the lack of government funds as they constantly argued. A committee was created—the main role of this group was to plan and implement a democratic electoral process with prudent timing.

The provisional junta of the government operated for a short time due to the inability of the members to reach any agreements. All of the proposals presented by the civilian members to pay heed to the demands of labour groups were rejected as the military members were more concerned about more radical issues and abused their privileges in proceedings. This resulted in the junta being dissolved completely and in the cabinet presenting its notice to dissolve. It was a return to the uncertain. The actions of the military were concentrated on going against the reactions of the people.

Acts of revolt began to form and the general public could do nothing but wait and expect the worst once again. Even though regular routines continued, other circumstances became part of daily routine—finding corpses on the streets had become normal, with nobody reacting; generally those murdered were teachers, students, labourers, farmers and union leaders; for every hundred bodies of humble people discovered, one body belonging to a member of a higher class was found.

Assassination of the Archbishop

In the critical moments of great tension and turmoil occurred an event that moved people worldwide: the Archbishop of the country was assassinated. He was celebrating the habitual mass in a small parish for nuns and at the moment when he raised his arms to present the body of Christ for communion, he received a bullet that was successful in ending the life of a man who had never hurt a thing in his entire life. Sprawled on the floor and on the brink of death, he used the last of his life energy to lament the fact that he was not able to finish his work on Earth. It was no secret to anyone who was responsible for this murder, on which grounds it was believed many years later, when a military officer died of cancer in the tongue, that this was divine punishment for having given the order to kill the Archbishop.

The Sunday prior to being killed, from the pulpit of the cathedral, the religious ministry had pleaded, implored, and even ordered the military forces to cease the repression of the people. This act angered military authorities and led to the shameless event to add to the thousands of other offences committed by this group. It was a gesture of desperation and incapacity that brought all moral values of the military to the ground, as this latest move had taken them to the lowest of the low.

Large protests became more frequent and heated as the Archbishop was seen by many as the only hope for salvation and was the sole instrument that served the good of the people. The media belonged to those of the higher, privileged classes and so, only that which benefited that group was made public. At an international level, the media was manipulated by the country's government, as it controlled what was released and attempted to defend a reputation that was getting harder and harder to conceal.

The church prepared the Archbishop's funeral—there was a mass held for the general public in front of the Cathedral. Amilkar, considering his religious values, decided to attend and positioned himself at the front of the crowd with some friends, students, and labourers. The celebration was about to conclude when the thousands of attendees were attacked from buildings nearby; the commotion was unanimous; people ran this way and that and at all sides one could see heavily armed soldiers. Amilkar and some colleagues that were near the wrought-iron fence jumped the gate and stayed in the basement of the church. Some of them had been beaten, others had been grazed by bullets, while still others had been trampled in their attempts to escape the attack.

Approximately five hours later, when all was calm again, international representatives of the Red Cross arrived and intervened to evacuate the group, but not before being searched thoroughly. Amilkar felt desolate when he saw the scene: where before the body of the Archbishop had lain and thousands of people had prayed, now lay destruction and only feelings of sadness, isolation, fear and rage remained, all overlapping and co-existing.

He arrived home at the precise moment when Meisa was listening to the news and it was said that "a guerilla group had hidden in the church with the intention of stealing the body of the Archbishop". This angered Amilkar and he told the family what had really happened—none of the information made public on the radio was true; the innocent were blamed in order to try and clean up the less-than-honest reputation of public security officers and the armed forces. The people felt abandoned. The only means which was available to present complaints, demands, the atrocities being committed by military groups and their allies to the general public, to humble and innocent communities, had now been destroyed. Going to mass or other religious ceremonies was no longer safe or secure. Any group activity was seen as threatening by armed forces and so, public group activities were controlled; celebrating graduations or having public events required special permission.

Worker and employee organizations in the middle class for their part increased their "activities" as well. Overtaking of public offices, churches and temporary work strikes became common ways of defending the rights of the working class. All of these activities were countered by security groups and by death squadrons, killing innocents just because they participated in work strikes.

Apparently the syndicates and the popular organizations were now the targets of the military and they attacked them with no mercy while the real culprits who were responsible for the destabilized economy and social strata enjoyed their wealth in places like Miami and other cities in the North.

Picture # 3.
One of the residences Where Amilkar used to live.

Amilkar did not stop his educative career and in spite of a neutral stand, he felt a lack of security for his family. In the last ten years he had had to move from house to house, neighbourhood to neighbourhood, every couple of years in light of the unsafe and threatening circumstances. On several occasions he had to stay temporarily at lodges set up by the Red Cross, especially when military groups decided to invade a zone, raid homes for weapons and use this as an excuse to arrest and kill people at random.

In one of those instances when there were rebels in a zone, the military surprised and attacked and neighbourhood in which Amilkar was living. The house was searched from top to bottom and they found nothing incriminating. He abandoned the area and started looking for another place to live. This was the fifth time in nine years he had to leave another home.

Another incredibly important event of the times that influenced Amilkar's life greatly was the suspension of work that lasted three days, decreed by the Federation of Workers. At the end of the three days a great protest occurred on all main streets of the city. This project also included to cancel all activities that involved education, commercialism and transport. In effect, the city found itself with no activity whatsoever in about 80% of its entirety, and an answer was expected from military authorities. On the third day about one hundred thousand people united on the streets according to international news. It ended with a speech from one of the leaders of the workers in central park. Surprisingly, government forces did not present themselves.

The next day, Amilkar went to work in his educational job as always and found that the students were in the hallways and the teachers were in an emergency meeting (as far as he was told). The meeting was being held by a military officer of high rank who administered the institution. Amilkar made to enter the room at the precise moment that the officer condemned the activities of the teachers and basically reprimanded those in attendance—Amilkar could not keep quiet and responded that teachers deserved respect for the sacrifices they made and that if thinking was a crime, then he would have to condemn the whole population in general, not just teachers, since all people were tired of the attacks from the military, a group that was not being punished in any way.

The officer was infuriated—he stood, looked directly at Amilkar and told him that from that day forth, he would face the consequences of his statements. He left immediately with his three guards, slamming doors as he left the building.

The environment was unstable and the principal suggested to Amilkar that he should take the rest of the day off. He went home taking the necessary precautions and decided that the next day, he would visit the Teacher's Association. He met with the directors and presented the events of the previous day. There was no question that Amilkar's life, and that of his family faced incredible danger.

They offered to apply for political asylum, but he figured that if he had to die, he preferred to do it in his own country. His friends and colleagues argued that his life and the life of his family were more important and that he was more valuable to them outside the country alive, than if he were another corpse in his own country.

To end that academic year, the students asked the principal for Amilkar to be recognized as the favoured teacher by all students at the celebrations to promote them to the next year of education. The graduation ceremony would be held in a theater in the city. The principal, for his part, invited the coronel to be seated at the head table. Amilkar sat with the students. When the principal implored him to join the head table, he responded that his place was with his students and that regardless, he would not sit at the same table as someone who violated human rights and that his place was with those that deserved his total respect and admiration.

A Decision That Forever Changed Amilkar's Life

Amilkar chose to pay heed to the advice of his friends who began the application process for his asylum and departure. During the last months, for security reasons, he spent his days with his family; he went out for personal errands only when absolutely necessary. He thought about the significance of abandoning his country.

One afternoon he received a letter that stated the exact day, time and place of destination for their departure. His family took the news with satisfaction—Amilkar did not share their sentiments and went to be alone in his room. He could not explain his feelings to himself. His thoughts were scrambled: leaving his country as a professional of education, abandoning a reputation he had developed over the last twenty years of work. On some occasions his students that were graduation had chosen him as their guide and had nominated him for promotions in school, as it was done in those years. That had been for him the best and highest honour a teacher could receive.

Time moved on, slowly but surely, and the day of the trip grew closer and closer. He considered making the move as though it were his life that was going on that trip. He left a note with a friend that was to be given to the principal of the institution two months after the trip, in which he communicated that for reasons he could not explain, he had to leave the country for an indefinite amount of time.

The night before he and his family were to leave he had a reunion with close neighbours—he distributed all of the family's belongings to them, including kitchen equipment, money, etc. The house was left to some friends and colleagues who would no longer have to worry about monthly rent—it was a gift that they had never expected. He asked for nothing in return.

At 4:00 am a bus arrived that would take the family to the airport. It came before dawn, in the dark, as if to capture a thief. There was no emotion in Amilkar. He meditated about why he had to leave his land, his friends and family. He had said his good-byes to his parents two days before. For Meisa, this trip represented tranquility. Done were the nights that she paced and paced, waiting for news of the events of the day. Ever since Amilkar started working as an educator and since the military began to take action against their activities, Amilkar's parents spent many days of bitterness and worry, to the point of supporting the decision to flee, preferring him to be far away and alive instead of in a cemetery as happened with many others during that time.

Whan, his father, did no more than hug him, being a strong man; he could not express with words what was in his eyes: a few tears that showed all the love for his son and the pain he felt at seeing him go, but still having strength to tell him that he felt he would never see him again. Amilkar left. He felt a great pressure in his chest and he would not look back. He wanted to disappear as soon as possible. He felt as though he were walking on air. He did not want his parents to go to the airport so as not to make the trip more difficult; however, saying good-bye to those that gave life is a pain beyond words, no matter the place or time.

His family boarded the bus; they seemed not to notice what or how much this meant for him. He was the last to get in. On the road, Amilkar saw the empty streets, closed shops protected by barricades, one or another person delivering daily bread, gasoline stations that were still closed. The shadows of the dawn protected him and he felt like an intruder trying to escape from the scene of a crime. The bus left the city limits and gained speed as it got on the highway. Amilkar looked at the scenery: the trees and some dark clouds that looked sad to see him go. He did not hear the conversations of the other passengers—he was completely engrossed in what he was leaving behind. His life would be no more than a memory. Another that abandoned the country. Even though his reasons were different, the simple act of leaving his country made him another immigrant, just like the rest. Some escaped because they had been in combat areas of the guerilla and the military and had survived miraculously; these were generally farm labourers that fled danger. Others travelled to protect their possessions; a third group just wished to advance economically, before the economic situation worsened, and took with them their finances to open up businesses or to invest in another country. Amilkar's motive was limited to the protection of his family. He was not afraid of death, had no money to invest, and was not in pursuit of a better job. Being a teacher was his life and his desire.

His older sister and two close friends that hated to see him go had made their way to the airport to say their good-byes.

Once at the airport and after several good-byes, the immigration representative that was with them showed them the documents without handing them over. Amilkar asked why and was told that it was merely a preventative measure to avoid having anyone try to stay in the USA. Amilkar walked away with a smile as he considered this trip to be forced on him and the USA was the least recommendable place for refuge. The same delegate gave all of their documents, passports, visas and identification cards at the window; then the family was sent to the immigration offices of the USA. Once all the tickets and documents were approved, they were guided to the doors of the airplane. Amilkar fixed his eyes on the natural beauty of his country, closed his eyes as if to record all those things that had been witness to his birth, growth, studies, work and almost the end of his life, to his memory. Their seats were assigned in the plane.

For some it was a regular flight; a business trip, a vacation, visiting family, etc. For Amilkar it seemed a trip with no return, his entire future in the hands of this departure. He was assigned a window seat to add to his torment. He could hear the noise of the motors but paid no attention. His children had been given separate seats and he felt alone. The plane ascended. The feeling of abandoning his country was latent. From the blue skies of his country he saw the beaches, plantations, the geographic structures, rivers, lakes and volcanoes. All of this scenery disappeared as the plane went higher and higher. Amilkar took with him all of his memories.

Physically he was distancing himself, but his heart stayed with his students, colleagues, friends, with whom he had always shared great moments. As Amilkar used to say, they made up his political and economic world and socially, they were the heat of a fresh cup of coffee or the first taste taken when out for a "couple of drinks" at some bar in the centre of the city.